The Princess and the Pea

MY VERY FIRST TEENY TINY
STRAWBERRY PAPERBACK
LIBRARY
Copyright © 1976 by One Strawberry Inc.
All rights reserved
Printed in the United States of America
Library of Congress Catalog Card
Number: 76-1502
ISBN: 0-88470-075-5

The Princess and the Pea

retold by
Maria Robbins

illustrated by
Diane Dawson

Once upon a time there lived a King and a Queen

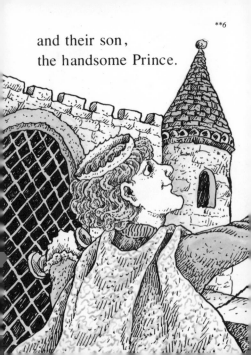

and their son,
the handsome Prince.

One day the King
and the Queen
said to the Prince,
"It is time for you
to get married.

You must find a Princess.''

The Prince saddled his horse,
and went to look
for a Princess.

He travelled
from one castle to another,

and saw one Princess,
and another.

But he did not
like any of them.

He came home very sad
and said,
"I have not found
a REAL Princess."

**21

One night there was a storm,
with thunder and lightning.

The King
and the Queen
and the Prince
heard a loud knocking
on the door.

The King
went to open the door,

and there
stood a Princess.

What a sight she was!
Water ran down from her hair
and her clothes.

But even though
she looked a mess,
the Prince liked her
and said to his mother,
"If she is a REAL Princess,
I will marry her."

The Queen ordered a bed
of twenty mattresses
made for the Princess.

Then she put a tiny pea
underneath all
the mattresses.

The Princess
tossed and turned
all night.

In the morning
she was black and blue.

"How did you sleep?"
asked the Queen.

"Very poorly,"
said the Princess.

"There was something very hard under my bed."

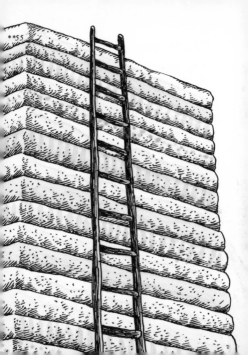
**55

The Queen kissed her
and said,
"You must be
a REAL Princess."

The Prince
and the Princess
were married,

and there was a big party,

because they were so happy
to have found each other.